Silence
By Lemniscates

Published by
MAGINATION PRESS
An Educational Publishing Foundation Book
American Psychological Association
750 First Street, NE
Washington, DC 20002

For more information about our books, including a complete catalog,
please write to us, call 1-800-374-2721,
or visit our website at www.apa.org/pubs/magination.

Graphic design by Lemniscates

Printed by Worzalla, Stevens Point, Wisconsin

Library of Congress Cataloging-in-Publication Data
Lemniscates.
Silence / by Lemniscates.
p. cm.
"American Psychological Association."
Summary: Simple text encourages the reader to be silent and listen for sounds
often not heard, such as the wind playing with a kite, or the chattering of trees.
ISBN 978-1-4338-1136-4 (pbk. : alk. paper) -- ISBN 978-1-4338-1137-1 (hard cover : alk. paper)
[1. Listening--Fiction. 2. Silence--Fiction.] I. Title.
PZ7.L53768Sil 2012
[E]--dc23
2011042529

Manufactured in the United States of America
10 9 8 7 6 5 4 3 2 1

By Lemniscates

MAGINATION PRESS · WASHINGTON, DC
American Psychological Association

In the silence

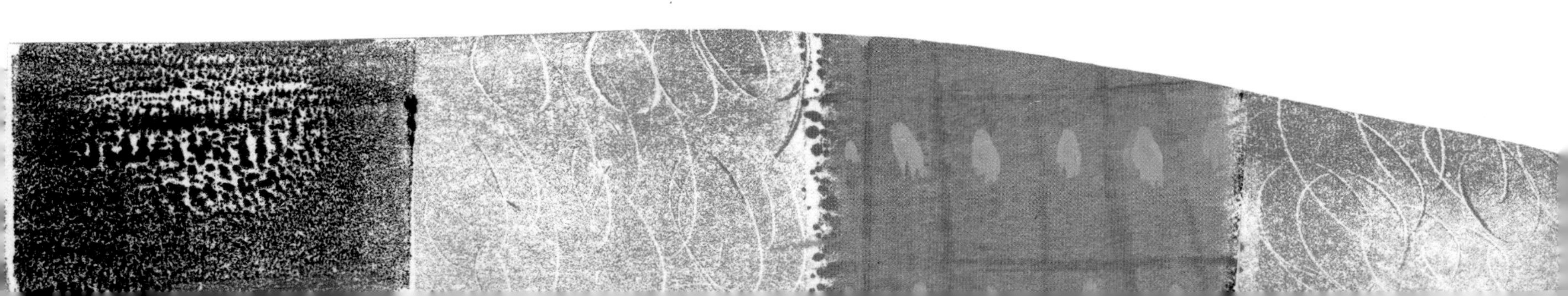

I can hear the waves crashing

And the wind playing with my kite.

At night, I can hear what the stars tell me

And in the morning, what the birds say.

When I listen, I can hear my feet when dancing

My heart when running

My legs when swimming

And my breath when still.

In Spring, I can hear bees loving flowers

In Summer, trees chattering

In Fall, leaves tumbling

In Winter, snow twinkling.

Be still.
Listen.
How many things can you hear?

Lemniscates is an illustration studio of artists and designers located in Barcelona. Their creative and imaginative books spark curiosity in children of all ages, and encourage children to develop their unique talents and skills for a deeper understanding of themselves and the world around them.

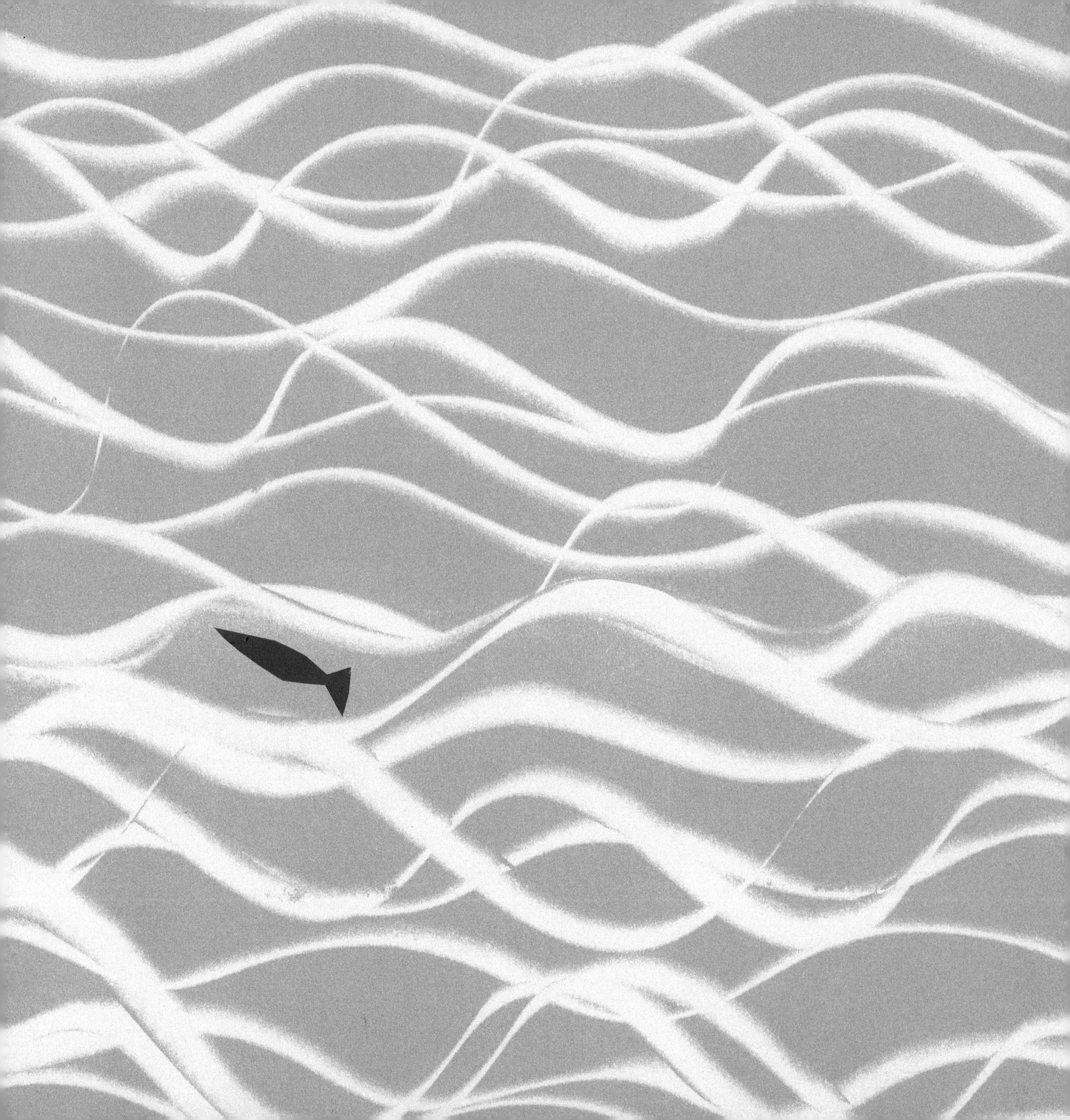